Hello Dolly

by
Mathu Hikkaduwa Liyanage

Printed in Victoria, BC, Canada.

ISBN: 978-1-4269-0805-7 (sc)
ISBN: 978-1-4269-0806-4 (e)

*Our mission is to efficiently provide the world's finest, most comprehensive book publishing
service, enabling every author to experience success. To find out how to publish your
book, your way, and have it available worldwide, visit us online at www.trafford.com*

Trafford rev. 11/20/09

 www.trafford.com

North America & international
toll-free: 1 888 232 4444 (USA & Canada)
phone: 250 383 6864 ♦ fax: 812 355 4082

Dedication

This book is dedicated to my loving wife, Soma Rani, who encouraged me, in many ways, to write the short stories; and for her undivided attention to my care and rehabilitation during a recent, prolonged illness.

Contents

Acknowledgements

My sincere thanks go to my daughter, Champika Karunanayaka of Townsville, Queensland, Australia, for typing the manuscript.

I should also thank my young grandson, Roshan Karunanayaka, a Year 11 student of the Pimlico State High School, Townsville, for designing the attractive front cover of the book.

I must also thank my younger grandson Sahan Thilakaratna, a Year 7 student of the Colonel Light Gardens Primary School, South Australia, for assisting me in computer work.

Blind Faith

It was just the beginning of summer – a season of sports, especially of cricket and enjoyment - barbeques, drinking, singing and dancing - in Australia.

Jack got up from bed to find that the whole room was lit up with bright sunrays streaking through the window panels and the yellow curtains with blue dots in the bedroom. He looked through the window, satisfied and elated, at the beautiful events that had been lined up for the day such as a good day's work in the office, the international cricket match between the Australian and English teams, and the birthday of Tony.

Tony Sirius always smartly dressed and with inquiring-type of eyes, was a reserved man. On the other hand, Jack Nelson was a playful and jovial person who is rather forgetful, and a dubious personality. Both of them worked in the Department of Postal Communications at Glenelg. They were good pals who studied at the Mitcham High School. Having passed the Higher School Certificate examination, they joined the Postal Department together as junior executive assistants. After about ten years both of them got married and settled down in Mitcham, which was close to their place of work.

Almost on every Friday after work, they used to go to the Glenelg Coronation Bar for a couple of beers before they went home. Both were good gossipers and their chitchats would go on for hours, and the amount of beer consumed also increased with every topic.

Jack found that Sharon, attractive blonde who was in her transparent pink pyjamas with a light blue floral design, still in sound sleep with her face partially buried in the silky pillow.

It was 7.30. Sharon also sensed that it was time to get up from bed and make the breakfast ready. Jack dressed in sunshine-yellow shirt and a light blue trouser sat at the breakfast table with Sharon, and enjoyed the cereals with milk, buttered toasted slices of bread, and drank a glass of orange juice to cap it all.

Jack with the office carry-case in one hand embraced Sharon with the other, and planted a warm kiss on her rosy cheek.

"Sharon, I will be late to come back tonight. I have a get-together party at the Orient Bar, Southern Square, Rundle Mall, after work. Today is Tony's birthday. The 20-over international cricket match will also be on the large screen of the restaurant," said Jack, before he left for work in the morning with a broad smile.

Immediately after work, both Tony and Jack walked fast to the restaurant to get a suitable table positioned by the screen to get a better view of the cricket match. From a distance they saw an illuminated signboard to get the message across, followed by yet another sign to say that the Orient band and the exotic dancers would be in attendance from 6 pm to midnight.

Tony and Jack occupied a two-seater table. After waiting for the main course for about 20 minutes, the topless waitress gave them a dessert menu:

Grand Mariner Tart: Succulent chocolate tart topped with Chantilly cream, chocolate and nuts S7.50

Universal Napoleon: Thin layers of phyllo pastry with diplomat cream and fruit preserves $7.50

Chocolate dipped Cannolis: Sweetened ricotta cheese filling $6.95

"Have you forgotten our dinner?" queried Jack with a reddened face. "Sorry Sir, this is a bar and not a restaurant," said the waitress with a broad smile across her chubby face. "All right, get us two plates of fish and chips, two bottles of Victoria Bitter, and a double J&B whiskey with soda."

Soon the plates were on our table. We started drinking and munching chips as people were crowding in and the band started tuning up their instruments. Loud music was later in the air, the hip dancers, some with over-painted faces, started their slow erotic movements to the shouts and clapping of the excited girls and boys in the bar. Most of them started dancing and singing in front of the stage, and the more matured drinkers watched them while getting on with their drinks and eating the snacks.

Sharp at 8.00, the cricket match was on the large screen and most of the heads moved that way, the English team batting and the Australian team fielding after the English captain won the toss. There was barracking and cheering for each of the scoring shots, and the fall of wickets made possible by fast and spin bowlers.

Surprisingly, a leg before the wicket (lbw), a controversial out was given to batsman Crawford without referring it to the third umpire for a decision. A commotion followed by shouting, arguments, throwing of bottles to the ground by the spectators and the play was stopped for ten minutes.

The commotion in the cricket grounds, as shown on the screen, made the audience in the bar get into wild arguments, shouting and thumping on tables.

Tony and Jack were cricket lovers and they were crazy over international one-day matches. The irony was that each of them supported the opposite teams. Tony barracked for the Australian team while Jack supported the English team. While they were watching the match on the large screen of the bar with a group of locals, both of them unconsciously argued over the leg before the wicket (lbw) out. They had an unusual flare up and got into a hot situation to insult each other, swearing and dragging even personal matters. The verbal exchange of words reached its climax when, all of a sudden, Tony said that one evening he saw Jack's wife with a younger man in the Glenelg beach, kissing each other.

Jack denied that his wife was not one of loose character. However, after about half an hour he admitted to Tony that there might be some truth in what Tony said because he found that his wife did not come home immediately after work. She was always late by about two hours. This happened, he said, about three days a week.

Tony suggested that Jack engaged a private detective to track down the movements of Sharon for a couple of weeks. Jack agreed. Both of them had another round of beer paid for by Jack, and left the bar as good, old friends.

Jack employed Tom Mansfield, a detective of the Allied Security Services, Pasadena, on a contract for three weeks at a cost of $2500. He followed Sharon from the bookshop on Allendale Street, Bowie, where she worked as a receptionist from eight to four every day. Tom found that Sharon went to the High Street Public Library, Hillside, worked in a cubicle usually hired by researchers to avoid disturbances from others attending the busy library. Tom also made confidential inquiries from the chief librarian and found that she came there for three days a week and would remain in the library for about two hours in the evening.

The library was in the leafy suburb of St Albans with ample space in the courtyard. The old granite building with moss marks on the walls was surrounded with huge trees, creating calm and serenity, an ideal place for those who followed their intellectual pursuits. It was the largest public research library in the State with a focus on South Australian information, and general reference material for information and research purposes.

Sign on the ground level, where general books and magazines were stacked, showed that the research section was upstairs on the second level.

At the ground level things were quite different. A couple of meters away from the escalator was the library section for children. It was like a beehive. Kids were reading, singing and reciting poems from books picked up randomly from the shelves. Some were making sketches of animals and birds on drawing boards hung on the side screens, partitioning the section.

A library, giving a fillip to intellectuals to research their topics, and providing children fun and joy appropriate to their age groups, was a boon to the members of the library and the community as a whole.

Tom stepped on to the escalator leading to the second level. He raised his eyebrows at the dead silence, which prevailed in this section. However, he held his breath and walked on tiptoe. He sat even in a cubicle. The cubicles were arranged in two rows, each having ten. Tom, in the cubicle, looked like a caged monkey gazing up and down.

Later in the evening, Tom followed Sharon until she went into her cubicle. With a smile across his face, he came out of the library. He lit a cigarette and puffed a few circles of smoke up in the air.

At the end of three weeks, Tom confided in Jack all what he had gathered. Highly relieved, Jack thanked Tom several times for his excellent work. Jack kept things to himself and did not even tell Tony about the findings of the investigation. He was still sceptical and watchful.

It was another bright summer day with a cloudless blue sky. Sharon got up from bed as happy as a lark because she knew that it would be a red-letter day for her. She was whistling and singing as if to say, 'Oh dear, today's my great day.' As soon as she saw Jack off to office, Sharon ran into the bathroom without stopping whistling her famous tunes, had a quick shower, and sprinkled her entire body with sweet-scented perfume. She wore a pink dress designed with tiny blue spots, and had light blue earrings to match. She got into her red sports car and was off to her bookstore for work as usual.

However, that day she found the work unusually boring, and was impatiently waiting to leave her workplace. The clock struck four. She jumped up from her seat and was in her car on the way to Peacock Printers, Dales Street, St Marys.

The owner and printer of Peacock Printers was, in fact, waiting for her to hand over the box of her printed novel, *It's not cheating.*

"Hi, Sharon, I am just waiting for you. Your novel has come out very well with the beautiful and attractive front cover you selected.It's a nice little book. Congratulations."

"Thank you."

As John placed the package of 150 books in the boot of Sharon's car, she wrapped up one book and left it on the front seat, as she left heading for her home.

Sharon parked the car, took the wrapped parcel and with glittering eyes and an enticing smile she rushed in to the lounge where Jack was seated, and presented the parcel to Jack.

Jack gave Sharon a warm hug and asked her, "Tell me what is in the parcel."

"Open and you will know what it is. It is precious."

Jack opened the parcel to find it was a book *It's not cheating* by Sharon Nelson, prized at $19.95. Jack turned a few pages to find that his name was also there as one the antagonists of the story.

Jack obviously overjoyed by Sharon's laborious and exciting work hugged her passionately, and sat down to tea.

Health is Wealth

Renato is a very organized individual who requires everything in life to be in order and in place. He dressed immaculately, well groomed, clean-shaven, and keen to be a methodical and perfect person.

He was equally conscious of health as well. He was very selective in what he ate as he knew that a healthy and balanced diet was the key to a disease-free life with longevity. He always avoided lean meat, but ate vegetables, green leaves, fresh fruits and fish with almost every meal. He was an advocate of mineral water but preferred chlorinated and fluoride tap water, because he thought animals, birds and insects that had access to up streams and waterways would contaminate mineral water, bottled and distributed to consumers by profit- oriented vendors.

A healthy man of 35 years, unmarried and living by himself in a boarding house in Mount Salvia close to his workplace, where he worked as the Engineer-in-charge of Water Resources of the Mount Salvia regional Council.

Somehow, Renato developed a crippling pain in the lower back. He disliked painkillers and relied more on herbal oils to relieve the pain, but it was like a yo-yo, going up and down all the time.

Renato met his General Practitioner who referred him to the Physiotherapy Department of the local hospital. He attended the clinic three days a week and regained his healthy life style and was back to normal work.

Back pain became a recurrent feature, and he attended the clinic off and on, though there was no ever-lasting cure.

One Sunday morning - a bright sunny day - Renato was reading the newspaper in the lounge when the telephone rang. Renato hurriedly picked up the receiver, and was quite surprised, but filled with immense joy, when he recognized that the voice was that of a girl quite familiar to him.

"Hello Reno, how are you? I heard from one of your friends that you are having some problems with your lower back? Are you all right?" came the sweetest voice from Thelma, Renato's girlfriend, with whom he had lost contact for sometime.

"I am OK, Love. I had a few problems with my lower spine and am undergoing a physiotherapy session at the hospital. These are very common ailments these days, and there is nothing to worry about."

"I am glad that everything is OK with you. But take care when you are especially at work. Do not lift things as you used to do. Will see you up in a couple of weeks. God bless you."

"Thanks a lot, Darling. Keep to your promise," a tearful Renato placed the receiver back with a heavy heart.

Renato spent the last few weeks with mixed feelings. He was delighted that Thelma contacted him after a long break but was unhappy about the back pain that had driven him to misery many a time.

Renato also noticed a slight pain in the abdomen, and a change in his toilet habits during the last few days. The slight cough he had was also persistent despite treatment.

He saw the General Practitioner as the pain was radiating from the back to the abdomen, and becoming worse. The doctor referred him to the Emergency Department of the hospital.

A doctor in attendance did an internal examination and found traces of blood in Renato's stools. He explained the situation to Renato but said, to make a correct diagnosis, it might be necessary to test the stools in a day or two. This was done and the tests confirmed that there was blood in the stools. A CT scan was later done followed up by a colonoscopy, which revealed that a polyp in the lower abdomen might be cancerous. A biopsy that was done two days later established that it was definitely cancerous and that the liver was also affected slightly.

Renato was later referred to the Cancer Clinic for chemotherapy. While he was under treatment, he was referred again for a bone scan. The scan revealed that three ribs were scarred. To make sure that the cancer had not spread to the bones, Renato had to undergo a PET/CT scan, which confirmed that no other organs were affected except the bowel and a small section of the liver. The Oncologist put Renato on six-chemotherapy sessions with the prospect of surgery to remove the diseased part of the liver and the bowel.

Renato was deeply distressed by the treatment program as he began to dislike the food he ate previously, had almost lost his taste buds, and the metallic taste he got when drinking water and fruit juices was awful. He was determined to fight the disease, and remained extremely positive.

He could not take away his mind from Thelma as he thought that, if she lived with him, things would take a better turn, but the question of giving her the information that he was suffering from cancer posed a problem for him.

Thelma used to give Renato a ring and inquired about his health quite often, and also discussed about their future.

One day, the telephone rang while Renato was having his breakfast – bacon and eggs with bread toast, and orange juice– and he immediately went to the phone and answered the call.

"Reno, I'm Thelma here. How are you? How is the back pain? Are you still attending the physiotherapy sessions?" These were the many questions Renato had to answer. She wanted to make sure that Renato had a clean bill of health.

Thelma dropped in at Renato's boarding house. As she got out of her car, Renato rushed in, gave her a fond kiss on her cheeks and led her to his room, which was tidy and clean.

" Oh, you are marvellous. With all your health problems, you seem to be doing very well," Thelma said directing her glittering eyes and a broad smile towards Renato, after surveying the room visually.

"Thelma, I feel sad and distressed to tell you that I have now been diagnosed as having bowel cancer following a series of tests and scans. I am undergoing six chemotherapy sessions with the possibility of surgery to remove the diseased part of the liver and the bowel. I really feel distressed and apathetic now. It's all the more severe as there is no one to help me in preparing the special diets I need, and to get over this crucial period of treatment," said Renato ruefully.

"Do not worry about it. I will be with you. Yes, you need assistance and support at this time. I know cancer is very common these days, and the earlier it is detected, the better are the chances of recovery," Thelma replied after embracing Renato and hugging him.

"I am extremely happy about your attitude and the stand you have taken in this matter. Good on you, Thelma."

"After about two weeks, they moved into a new house with Thelma by his side.

Months rolled by after the successful surgery, and Renato was on his way back to his normal life. As a matter of gratitude and their flourishing love towards each other, they decided to marry as soon as possible.

Both of them were making arrangements for their modest wedding, when in a flash car accident, Thelma died most unexpectedly while they were returning home from a shopping spree.

Back to almost square one, Renato could not get over the loss of her darling Thelma for quite some time. In the nights of clear blue sky, Renato would gaze at the galaxy of stars to find out whether there was any new star born.

Chuti

Priscilla was only five years old when Chuti came to her home to replace the lovely Blacky who died about three months back from a leg injury, despite continuous care and treatment during her illness.

Chuti was just like Blacky with shiny, glossy, black hair. Even her eyes were covered with hair, which prevented her from finding her way sometimes. I did not know why nature created such handicaps. Perhaps it may be for the protection of eyes from light.

Chuti was well looked after by Priscilla who did all the bathing, brushing, feeding and putting her to sleep at night. As soon as Priscilla came from school, she would pat, hug and stroke her head, ear and back before she started her school homework.

Even when the other members of the family were at the front door, she would start barking and go to the front door to see who the visitor was. She was a very keen watchdog by breeding.

It is a different situation when Priscilla came home from school or any other outing. She would not bark but cry in a dragging, sad voice, and jumping at her until Priscilla patted and hugged her.

Chuti, at the age of 14 years, developed heart problems and found difficulty in breathing. She was taken to the Veterinary Surgeon who said to Priscilla that her condition was bad and that it could not be cured. Either she should be under treatment for the rest of her life or she should be put to sleep by an injection.

Priscilla, almost in tears, accepted the first option. She brought her home, put her in bed and nursed her, often stroking and hugging.

One morning, Priscilla heard a horrific groan from the room where Chuti was resting.

Priscilla rolled her eyes and cried out as loud as she could, "Is she all right?"

Chuti had entered into her death agony. Her breath becoming faster with a rattling sound, making her sides heave. Her whole body trembled. There were bubbles of froth at the corners of her mouth.

Priscilla, who could not face up to the situation, ran back into her room and watched Chuti, with tears flowing down her rosy cheeks as fresh as a rosebud that had just cracked.

A slight breeze bringing in a sweet-scented smell of flowers from the hedge of lavender right round that part of the house wafted through the corridors and into her room as if to console her. Priscilla opened her nostrils wide and breathed it in a mystical sensuous fervour.

Priscilla closed her eyes creating Chuti's image in front of her. Her lips wavered and eyes filled with tears. Her heart started to beat slower and slower, fainter and fainter, in contrast to Chuti's, which worked in the opposite direction.

Priscilla ran up to Chuti's bed. Chuti was struggling to breathe. Finally, she closed her eyes partly and breathed her last breath. She was dead.

Priscilla, in a burst of uncontrollable crying and sobbing, held the body of Chuti to her well-developed breast, and prayed that she could see her in her dreams, hovering above her head.

The Blue Skies

"Herman, it is January 1 today; another year has passed. I feel life is boring and almost empty. I do not know how I could spend the rest of my life like this," said the beautiful Joanne, the disgruntled wife.

"I can understand you darling, but both of us are helpless in this situation. People say life does not provide you with what you want or ask for. It's seldom it happens. We cannot go against nature. We will have to put up with it," said Herman philosophically.

"Herman, you can say so, but I am the person who is penalized. If not for the position I hold at my workplace, which keeps me fully occupied, life is not really worth living."

Joanne is an Executive Director and a Board Member of the giant Lees and Lords Engineering firm, drawing a salary of $250,000 per year, besides bonuses. She is beautiful and smart.

Herman is handsome, intelligent and alert, and owns a chain of fashion stores, making him one of the richest persons in the community.

Their 3-storied, modern mansion with 10 rooms and the well paved and a well-planned garden is indeed a head-turner. The mansion is beautifully painted with light sea blue and all the rooms pink – a wish of Joanne fulfilled. Besides, it has a large swimming pool, and when lit up in the evenings, it looks a classic design with its blue water like a lagoon.

Herman and Joanne own and possess everything they like, and lead a very luxurious life. But they lack one precious thing – a child.

Both of them have been treated for infertility and undergone a series of tests but without success. They do not want to adopt a child from overseas because the process is long-drawn out.. They have no problems with money but they are concerned with the nerve-wracking delays. They do not like a surrogate mother on ethical grounds, although there are so many willing to rent a womb for $25,000 to $50,000 for the purpose.

"Joanne, I am sure the fertility drugs you are taking will prove to be effective, and, one of these days, you might conceive."

"Yes, I am hoping against hopes," replied Joanne with a glance at Herman.

Herman drew Joanne closer to him, kissed and hugged her in an attempt to console her.

To get away from the boredom and to take a break away from work, Joanne one day suggested that they went on a long holiday. Herman who was equally anxious to do so grabbed the idea and made arrangements to travel round the world.

Herman and Joanne went to the airport, and soon they were in their first lap of the journey.

Seated in First Class, they were enjoying an expensive wine, arm in arm, like a newly married couple in their honeymoon.

All of a sudden, Joanne developed a slight back and stomach pain, and was in the toilet off and on.

Although Joanne was having contractions and her waters had broken, she was adamant that she was not pregnant.

The crew was alerted, and they went through the list of passengers to find out whether there were any doctors on board. Luckily, they found the name of a doctor, Nesta Anderson. She immediately examined Joanne and found her 9 cm dilated, and there was little time to waste.

The most upsetting factor was that the baby was in the breech position, which invariably requires a caesarean birth.

To Dr Anderson, it was bizarre. She could not believe it was happening.

When Dr Anderson questioned Joanne about her back pain, she said that she went to the toilet and passed lot of water. Dr Anderson told the crew who had assembled that they were going to have a baby soon. A flight attendant offered to boil water and get warm blankets, but Anderson told her that such things happened only in movies.

Dr Anderson was wandering what was going to happen if the baby was not breathing or the mother bleeding, and whether the crew would give her a plastic knife if she would have to take the baby out. However, Dr Anderson kept her cool even cracking jokes despite the tension-filled cabin.

With the baby already on the way, Dr Anderson was forced to perform the delivery on board next to the cabin and the toilets.

The crew screened off the First Class, and moved Joanne to a seat with her head against the window. With a few stunned crewmembers watching on, Dr Anderson guided the tiny, cute baby named, Star, into the world in a matter of minutes. The baby was given an emergency mask as a precaution but she had no breathing difficulties.

Sutures were used to tie the umbilical cord, which was cut with scissors shortly after.

Dr Anderson held the baby by her legs and kept her on mum's stomach.

The delighted and relieved crew asked Dr Anderson what they should do now.

"Take photos," said Dr Anderson with a chuckle.

Joanne breast-fed the baby for the remainder of the journey, which took 2 ½ hour period.

The crew told Dr Anderson that they would land ahead of time to which she said that they would have got a speed fine if there were cameras in mid-air.

The crew sent congratulatory messages to mum with a bundle of pink flowers, as the medical team was boarding on touchdown.

The Airlines did not ignore Dr Anderson for her noble act. They upgraded her ticket to First Class, and presented her with a bottle of red wine and a box of French perfumes.

Mr and Mrs Herman were rushed to a lavish 5-star hotel close to the airport for the night with the "precious treasure" they now possess and own.

Following morning, Mr and Mrs Herman sent a bunch of flowers, perfumes and chocolates to Dr Anderson with the message that both she and Star were doing well and calling her "my angel".

Hello Dolly

John Till was a friend of mine from our school days when we were studying at Glenelg High School. We lived close to each other, and that closeness still remains intact. Now 35 years of age, John is a sheep farmer. A stocky, well-built man; always a good talker then, and even now. Whenever I found free time, I used to go to this farm and chat for hours and hours on any subject that crept into our minds. John possessed a wealth of information about global warming, cloning, stem-cell research, and was knowledgeable of the current downturn trend of the US economy, spreading to other countries in the world. He seemed particularly interested in the fast growing trade giants, China, India and other Asian countries, which have a great impact on world finances.

John was so interested in gathering information about various current topics; he would never miss a lecture delivered by any eminent politician, economist or health and welfare expert who came to town.

"Hi John, good evening," I said as I entered his farmhouse. He sat in an armchair on the verandah, puffing a tobacco-pipe and sending circles of smoke in the air like a teenager who wanted to demonstrate his ingenuity.

John got up from his seat immediately after he saw me, came up to me and shook hands, holding my hand tightly. "Good to see you, Steve."

As we sat for a chat, he brought out a tin of biscuits and a bunch of bananas, and placed them on the coffee table. We gossiped for a while over a hot cup of steaming coffee, and later walked around the block of land on which the solidly built stone house stood.

The house was on a hilltop, very rocky and barren except two gum trees standing near the verandah, giving much needed shade in the warm evenings. It presented an exciting landscape at the distance with the sunset at the background, and steep mountains almost touching the blue skies, so blue the color itself provided pleasure.

A lean waterfall, thin due to the prevailing drought, glided down between rocks like a snake recently shed of its skin.

Beyond the farmhouse, stretched the sheep farm with a flock of about 250 sheep. They moved without looking at each other, eating whatever they could find before being herded into their enclosures for the night.

Both John and I sat on a rock, and enjoyed the scenery, the sight of sheep, their characteristics and the way they behaved.

The soft, cold evening breeze brought in a sweet scent from the wild flowers around the farm, thankfully overpowering the strong smell of sheep.

As we sat on the rock, I saw a strong ram coming towards us with a younger, neat and clean ewe, followed by the flock.

The ram addressed the ewe as Miss Dolly Jnr., and then said, "You look exactly like Dolly – the world's most famous sheep - who was cloned in 1996".

"Yes, I do."

"Why is your counter-part called Dolly?"

"Because Dolly was cloned from a part of a mammary gland. She was named after the busty, country western singer Dolly Parton.

"But you aren't very busty".

"I guess, but they'll develop soon, and then, you'll be after me all the time."

"Yes, it'll be interesting." The jolly good ram, Bully, then asked, "Do you know who created Dolly Sr.?"

"She was cloned by Dr Ian Wilmut, Keith Campbell and colleagues at the Roslin Institute in Edinburgh, Scotland.

"Oh dear, so men can create animals? But, who created man and woman in the first case?"

Miss Dolly hesitated, and then said, "People say it was God who created the first man and woman – Adam from the dust of the earth, and Eve from Adam's rib –."

"Isn't that funny? Is God a man, then?"

"I cannot exactly answer that. That's what people say. But, God is not here to question. It must be a belief, I suppose, coming down generations."

It was getting darker, and a strong wind blew across the farmhouse making awful sounds. John and I hurried inside, and sat down for a glass of Victorian Bitter Beer, which was the popular drink at the time.

Now John took over the conversation of Dolly Jr. and Bully from the point where they had stopped, and commented, "Steve, wasn't that conversation sensible and meaningful?

"Absolutely."

"John, what do you really mean by cloning?"

"It's a laboratory method of producing cells or even offspring almost genetically identical to a single person or animal. That's why people called Dolly a copy of her mother."

"I understand it now. But what is it that people call therapeutic cloning. I hear talk about it all the time?"

"It's a technique to produce cloned embryos, which create stem cells that can, in turn, be used to repair damaged or defective tissue in the parent of the cloned cells. Unlike cloning, it does not produce cloned animals or human babies"

"So, why all this fuss about therapeutic cloning? It's so useful in treating people with Alzheimer's or Parkinson's disease, and when such stem cells could even be used to grow replacement livers or hearts or any of a variety of organs for transplant without fear of rejection?"

John shrugged, "People will always oppose any new technique whether it's useful or not. In this case, people oppose it on religious and ethical grounds. They may have good reasons for it."

The following morning, John and I sat in the verandah enjoying a morning cup of coffee when we spotted Dolly and Bully coming out of their enclosures, engaged in conversation just like the previous evening.

"Dolly", said Bully, "You're just like your mother."

"Sure, because I'm cloned. It's really disgusting at times. I'm revolted because I am living with my mother who is exactly like myself. When friends come to meet me, they can't distinguish between my mum and me, and they sometimes mistake my mum for me. They giggle when they realize that they've made a mistake. Such situations drive me crazy because they affect my self-respect and dignity."

"Yes, I can see that."

"Not only that Bully, I'm afraid I might develop some abnormal ailments and die sooner than others my age."

"Why do you say that?"

" Because the original Dolly developed arthritis and a progressive lung disease. Sadly she passed away prematurely. This knowledge takes the life out of me."

"Dolly, those are psychological problems and you must keep them out of your mind, and try to lead a normal life. I have heard a story that a young chubby girl wearing a low-cut top challenged a Chess Champion for a contest. They played but, to the surprise of every one who watched the game, the champion lost the match. When asked what led to his downfall, the champion said with a subdued smile that he used to see "doubles" on the chess board."

"Yes, it's easy to preach."

"Dolly, imagination and wild thinking can run riot, and make you very unhappy. So, try to keep it all out of your mind. You'll be okay."

Dolly and Bully walked past us to their grazing grounds while John and I retreated to the dinning room to have our breakfast – toasted bread, bacon and two "bull's-eyes" prepared out of fresh farm eggs, and a strong cup of coffee.

The Tempest

Dean and Lorna were a devoted couple who married about five years ago after a romantic life. Though Lorna was playful, she resigned to her new role and responsibilities as a good housewife.

Before the marriage, Lorna had a long and steady relationship with Andrew who eventually married another girl whom he met at work. Lorna and Andrew remained friends.

Dean was a tractor driver. Living in farmlands, he found his job provided him with ample opportunities to earn lot of money. He was fairly rich and a disciplined person who did not over-step boundaries in any thing.

Lorna was quite happy as a housewife, and kept the house and garden nice and clean. She was conscious of what food they ate, and good nutritious food was always on the table.

Their son, Bobby, a three-year old, was cute and precious to them. They looked after him well. Bobby, in turn, loved his parents so much that he became upset when mum and dad were out of sight even for a few minutes.

It was winter but, as a result of global warming, the pattern of weather had taken an incredible turn for the worse that even weather readers on TV could not forecast the weather correctly most of the time.

Dean thought that today would be another wet and stormy day although there were intermittent flashes of sunrays reaching the earth. To buy some groceries that they had run short of, Dean and Bobby left for the shop not far away from their house.

Dean finished his shopping and was about to come home when torrential rains and a fierce storm started to unravel Nature's ferocity.

Lorna was gathering clothes from the clothesline in the backyard. She found it difficult to maintain her equilibrium because of the sudden gust of wind, which even uprooted several tall trees in the garden.

"Hello Lorna, what are you doing?" came the words to her surprise. It was Andrew who stepped into the verandah after tying his horse to a tree in the front yard.

"You are welcome, Andrew. In fact, I did not see you for sometime."

"I was busy these days. I saw you in the shopping centre one day but I was too busy to talk to you."

The rain was pelting on the verandah and both of them had to put planks and rolls of clothe against the door spaces to prevent water coming into the house.

Lorna and Andrew went inside the house and sat in the lounge and started chatting.

Andrew noticed that Lorna had gained extra weight and now a fuller figure than five years ago when they broke up. She had lost nothing of her vivacious features – the glittering blue eyes had not lost their melting characteristics, the dishevelled hair by the wind and rain kinked stubbornly about her ears.

All the time, Lorna was concerned about her child and was very anxious he came home soon. She stood near the window and wiped away mist that had collected on the windowpane with a piece of cloth so that she could have a clear view.

The rain and wind was furious as a gust of wind coming through the window struck her face. She covered her face with her hand and stepped back to fall into the stretched arms of Andrew who was just behind her. Andrew looked into Lorna's face and her trembling body aroused Andrew's all time infatuation and craving for her flesh. He pushed her hair back from the face, which was hot and steamy. Her lips appeared like a slice of watermelon moist and reddish. Excited Andrew saw nothing he could do other than getting her lips together and to kiss her over and over again.

As Lorna lay in his arms, Andrew touched her whiter, full breasts, which gave themselves up in a shattering rapture. He looked at her mouth that was a fountain of euphoria.

Andrew lay upon her breathless, dazed and his heart beating like a hammer against her tender, mellow body.

The rain was over and the storm receded. There was sunshine again coming through the spaces in the wooden wall, making the house brighter and lit up.

Lorna came to the verandah and saw Andrew ride away.

Now Lorna was waiting for her son and hubby who, she thought would be drenched but they had avoided the rain and the storm.

Lorna had set the table for dinner. They sat at the table and had a few drinks of French wine – their favourite – and ate dinner.

Everyone was happy now that the treacherous rain and wind had disappeared.

Opals Vs. Diamonds

In the village town of McLaren Valley, mostly a wine producing region with vineyards all round, the families of Opal and Diamond lived side-by-side for generations, competing with each other in the production and sale of wines. Both families had wine cellars, wine stores and pubs teeming with locals and visitors to the town in the evenings.

It became almost a weekly practice of the Diamond to display a notice showing the price of wines less than what was listed in the Opal's Stores. It was the wife of Diamond, who owned the Diamond's Wine Store, recorded the details of the events daily in her diary, even including price reductions.

There were frequent arguments over this issue but to no avail. The competition in prices continued unhindered as normally happened in a competitive society.

I was about ten years old when I began to notice the unusual characteristic of my father who, for the slightest thing that annoyed him, banged on the well-polished cellar door saying, "Diamonds are alligators" in a loud and powerful voice.

No one knew what it was all about and I, as a child, was not surprised, but the hate against the Diamonds began to take root in me although I did not take it seriously.

People say that such traits are passed on to children by their parents, and it is true with limitations. But, two of my daughters acquired such habits from their peers and the people around them for which I cannot be blamed. However, I should have taken precautions to ensure that my daughters kept company with a selected lot of peers and moved about in better surroundings.

One day, I heard my mother telling father that she wanted to go to a shop trading in diamonds to get her diamond in the pendant adjusted. He became so furious that he banged the door and yelled out, "Do not go to any shop trading in diamonds; they are alligators."

As I grew up, father gave me slight clerical work at the office of the wine store. He also gave me a few coins at the end of the day for pocket money. I was really delighted about it. My work in the office became more frequent after school hours, the work being both enjoyable and profitable.

Over a period of time, I noticed a young, handsome man who came to the wine store almost regularly to buy wines. My father, in fact, questioned him whether the wines were for him. His straightforward reply was, "No, it's for my father who is wine-lover."

One day, I came face to face with this man, who introduced himself to me as "Carlo." He had a broad smile on his clean-shaven face. "Excuse me," he said, and asked me, "Love, have you any boy friends?"

"No".

"Even at school?"

"No," I said, looking direct into his piercing eyes.

Days passed by. Carlo's visits became more frequent. He was now browsing the stocks of wine stocked at the shelves more than buying them – Napa Valley Proprietary Red Wine, Napa Valley Syrah, Russian River Pinot, California Red Wine, Bigi "Secco" Orvieto Classico, Penfolds Yattarana and Grange Red Wines - a few selected varieties.

One day, Carlo suggested that we get together. It was a surprise to me as I had just passed my sixteenth birthday. I told my younger sister about it and she gave me her full support, as siblings always endeavour to help each other when they were under pressure or in trouble.

My mother had noticed our relationship and, when I posed the question to her, she said she would discuss it with father and let me know their decision, as it was customary to get the blessings of parents for marriage by young couples. I got the consent of both parents, and we started living together with my parents, as they thought that we could understudy the running of a wine store and take over the entire ownership of the business once they passed away.

Both of my parents died of flu, which ravaged the whole town. They were 60 years and 55 years old when they died. Carlo and I became the joint partners of the thriving business, as my parents wished.

Later, I found out, to my utter disappointment, that Carlo had an affair with a teacher in a primary school for over 10 years. Finally, he eloped with her and lived in New Zealand.

My two daughters, Cordelia and Catalina, grew up fast. They proved to be a big asset to me in running the business.

At a National Wine Seminar held in the Adelaide City Centre, I bumped into a nice looking, well-groomed man in a light blue striped woolen suit and a red tie. He had a steaming cup of coffee in one hand and a seminar docket in the other. He sat by my table and asked me, " How is the seminar progressing? Do you enjoy the proceedings?"

"Yes, very informative and useful".

He had a nametag 'Renato Diamond' tacked on to his shirt. I noticed him reading my nametag 'Felicia Opal' pinned on my frock.

"By the way, how are your two daughters? I heard they are settled down. Aren't they?"

"Yes, my eldest daughter Cordelia lived with a man for about five years until he left her for a much older, attractive woman. She has two children, a son and a daughter. They are living with me."

"Catalina is also married to one Teo Terencio who has a chain of fancy dress shops. They are both doing well."

It reminded me that Cordelio had a long affair with Colin Diamond when they were in high school. My husband strongly objected to the relationship, as he also hated the Diamonds for their unacceptable behaviour towards our business. Although I had an impartial attitude towards the relationship, I was forced to toe the line with Carlo lest it would have soured our own relationship. I should have, however, taken a bolder and an independent stand, as it was mainly a human relationship issue and not really concerned with the business. I knew that Colin was highly disturbed and upset over his failure to win over Cordelia. He still remained unmarried.

"Renato, I read in the newspapers that your wife died of a freak car accident recently. I wanted to send you a card of condolence but again …"

"Yes, Felicia, I can understand you. Kathy was a very lovely woman and a devoted wife and a loving mother to my daughter and three sons. I miss her badly."

"Felicia, I think people are re-assembling at the seminar hall. I have to get back soon as I am leading the group on 'Wine Sales.'"

"OK, we will meet soon."

Renato had such a striking and forceful personality; I could not take my eyes away from him even when the seminar was in session. There was something different in him from other men. I could not really express that feeling in words. I loved him so much that I felt that I was under a spell.

Back in the wine store, I could not really concentrate on my work. To add to more, the sales of wine were dwindling and even the pub was less patronized now because of the price-cutting tactics of the Diamonds, even on beer.

I could not believe the figures and I was re-checking the registers when the telephone rang. I jumped at it thinking that it was from one of our wine distributors. It was not to be.

"Felicia, Renato here. Are there any others around you?"

"No, no, why?"

"I would like to take you for a cup of coffee this evening. Will it be all right with you?"

"OK, I will meet you at the shopping centre in front of La Sales Drapery Store."

"Right, I will see you around 6.30."

'What a blessing in disguise, after all!' I thought to myself. It will give me some sort of relief from this persistent headache caused by the downturn of our wine sales.

Getting out of the store at that time was a problem for me as Cordelia and Catalina would be in the store to assist me in the transactions. I pinned my faith and hopes on Angela, a reliable and sincere friend of mine from our school days.

"Angela, it is Felicia here. Will you please come to the store at about 6.00 and pick me up? If Cordelia and Catalina happen to be at the store at the time, please tell them that you are taking me to meet a wine distributor who is in town. I will tell the story behind this when we meet."

"OK Felicia; don't worry, I will be there."

It was a bit cold evening though it was still late autumn. It was getting darker and cooler – an ideal time to be in the arms of a lover with a steaming cup of coffee just in front of you. My imagination started to fly more than the speed of a jet.

I had my dress ready so that, as soon as Angela came, I could dress up for the occasion and make the first move.

Cordelia and Catalina turned up as usual and were checking the registers and attending to the work at the counter.

"Hello Felicia," Angela jumped out of the car and embraced me as she stepped into the store. She also waved to Cordelia and Catalina who were busy with their work.

Catalina sprung from her seat and walked towards Angela, inquiring about the purpose of her visit at this unusual busy time of the evening. Angela explained to her that she wanted to take her sister to meet a popular wine distributor who was in town. Catalina appeared pleased about what was said and went back to her seat.

Felicia and Angela were now on their way to the shopping centre.

Felicia related the whole story to Angela, and about Renato. Angela listened intently and asked Felicia, "Are you sure that every thing is ok?"

"Absolutely, I am madly in love with him. This is the first time I found what real love is. He is the nicest man I have ever met in my life so far," said a beaming Felicia.

"OK, but take care," said Angela after dropping Felicia in front of the La Sales Drapery Store.

Renato, who was waiting for Felicia, ran up to her. "Oh dear, it is lovely to see you again." He gave a hug and led Felicia to the nearby coffee house. They sat at a table under candlelight. They sipped their coffee, chatted, and started kissing and touching each other for sometime.

Every touch of Renato gave Felicia a sort of an electric jerk that kept her every nerve trembling with excitement and love. They started kissing on the forehead, the neck, the cheeks, and the lips for so long that they forgot about the clock clicking away. It was 10.00 when Renato called a taxi to send Felicia back to her wine store to cover up their tryst from Cordelia and Catalina.

As Felicia entered the store, Cordelia and Catalina gathered around her inquiring whether it was actually a wine distributor or a wine seller that she met, as they recollected how Felicia had told them on an earlier occasion how she casually met Renato Diamond at a seminar. Both of them teased Felicia and requested her not to fall into the trap of Diamonds – the alligators. Catalina was more vociferous than Cordelia in their insinuations.

"Do not worry, dear. I am quite aware and mindful of the situation," Felicia said, to dispel any suspicion in their minds about an affair with Renato.

Days rolled by quickly as meetings between Felicia and Renato occurred quite often to such a point that it became quite impossible to separate them, despite the animosity and hatred that existed between the families of Diamonds and Opals.

Felicia would often go out in the evenings and come late at night. Catalina sensed that, and wanted to get down Felicia's ex-husband Carlo from New Zealand to instill some sort of sense into Felicia's to correct her erratic behaviour, which was detrimental to the family of Opals. It was the intention of the Diamonds to buy over the business of Opals at any cost and set up one establishment to cover the businesses of both families.

When Felicia came back to the store from a late night out with Renato, she found, to her surprise, Carlo having a nap in the couch of her lounge-room. Carlo got up from the couch addressing Felicia, "Hi dear, how are you? It's a long time since I saw you last."

"Yes, it's nice to see you. But, what brought you here after so long?"

"I came just to warn you that you are playing into the hands of Diamonds who are keen to take over our business, and for them to flourish as the leading wine dealer in the town. I warn you not to give in to the Alligators. This is the last warning I give to you." He banged the door and left.

In the heat of these controversies and hatred, the mother of David Diamond – the owner of the Diamond wine stores – died suddenly of pneumonia. All the stores, shops and business places in the town closed on the funeral day as a mark of respect for the traditional Diamond family. Only the Opal's store was kept opened despite the appeals of Felicia and Cordelia, reminding them of *nil nisi bonum – nothing but good of the dead*. Catalina and her husband together with Carlo and his partner opposed the closure of the store vehemently. However, it was agreed later in the day to attend the funeral.

Felicia, Cordelia, Catalina and her husband, Carlo and his partner attended the funeral services. After the services and other rituals were over, the Diamond family members invited them to their house for tea.

Whilst thanking the Diamonds for their invitation, the Opals said that they would certainly visit them in about a month's time, as they thought that it was not the right time for a visit, as any likely heated arguments might disturb the solemnity of the occasion.

On the day arranged for the get-together, the members of the Diamond family warmly welcomed the Opals when they stepped into their home. After exchange of pleasantries, they sat down for chitchat over biscuits, cakes, tea, coffee and wines they excelled in producing and selling. In the midst of their lively conversations, Sue, the daughter of Renato Diamond, brought the diary kept by her deceased grandmother and started reading extracts from it which revealed that Felicia's father had a long affair with her but, as he appeared to be a playboy, she gave him up, giving rise to the hate between the two families. The diary also revealed that the relationship between Colin Diamond and Cordelia was broken up by the objections raised by the Opals family, leaving Colin a confirmed bachelor. All looked stunned, some showing surprise, a few shedding tears of sorrow and joy.

Felicia and Renato took the initiative to show their attachment to each other by kissing and hugging while Colin and Cordelia locked themselves in each other's arms, kindling a dormant love. There were loud applause, cheers and appreciation from others, burying the long-standing hatred between the two clans – the Diamonds and the Opals.

Heating Up

At the time of the tsunami of 2004, I was residing with my family at Unawatuna, meaning, "there it fell," a beautiful wide curving golden beach about 5km south of Galle, the second regional capital of Sri Lanka.

The beach protected by coral reef provided safe swimming, wreck and reef diving. It also had several surf points, making Unawatuna a more popular travel destination.

On the Boxing Day, when the tsunami ran through the coastal belt of South East Asia, Unawatuna was seriously affected by the destruction of hotels, boats and sporting gear that was stacked in sport stores, disrupting the orderliness of the town. Some holidaymakers were also swept away by the tsunami tidal waves.

The resilient residents came through one of the worst natural disasters as quickly as the onset of the tsunami, mainly due to the efforts of volunteers, government agencies and the rich, who supported the cause immensely.

One of them was Newton Cabraal, the richest in the town who had a chain of hardware stores. My house was close to his mansion. Both of us always got together and enjoyed the beautiful evenings over a few glasses of beer. The colourful sunset in the foreground, beyond the peaceful sea, made the evenings highly attractive. We engaged ourselves in useful conversations about global warming and its repercussions on the world as a whole, and sea erosions devastating the low-lying areas.

One evening when Newton visited me as I was on the verge of packing up and leaving Unawatuna for a property on higher ground, I asked him what global warming really meant, out of curiosity.

"It is the long term average rise in near Earth surface temperatures – basically, it means that the atmosphere is getting hotter," Newton said confidently, sending a cloud of smoke from the manila cigar he was puffing.

"Do you think it can be controlled?"

"Certainly. Man and animals are the two main causes. In the past every warming and cooling event has been due to natural causes and the role of greenhouse gases has been significant in determining our climate. These gases trap Earth's atmosphere and keep it at a habitable temperature, they are effectively the planets insulation, without which we cannot live. When we increase the amount greenhouse gases in the atmosphere, the insulative effect increases, which we, of course, cannot avoid. We are currently producing 14 times the greenhouse gas that nature can handle and this excess is accumulating in the atmosphere. We need to reduce our greenhouse gases dramatically to prevent global warming."

"You said that animals also produce emissions. How is that?"

"Paul, you would be surprised to hear that sheep and cattle also produce greenhouse gas emissions, rivaling other major contributors such as industry and motor vehicles because of the methane they emit orally."

"I hear people say that Antarctica will also be affected by global warming. Is it correct?"

"Oh yes, global warming could melt Arctic's ice as early as 2040, raising serious environmental as well as commercial and strategic issues, according to modeling done on supercomputers. It could change the world's ecosystem including sea and surface life, weather and shipping patterns, the sea-level rise, changes in availability of fresh water, the increasing incidence of floods, droughts and hurricanes."

"Newton, I am concerned about sea-level rise. Will it certainly affect the people living in low-lying areas close to the sea?"

"Certainly, there is no second word about it."

"That's the reason I have bought a property on highland and making arrangements to move out as early as possible."

"Think over it seriously before you make any move, as your tourist business will be greatly affected by such a move especially at this time when tourism is making such great strides," Newton said, as he was leaving.

Nevertheless, I went ahead with my plans to move. My friends and relatives flocked the house from morning, interrupting at times my work. The removal trucks came on time and the removalists started loading the trucks. The news of my leaving the town spread like wild fire in the tiny town of Unawatuna. Newton, who had returned from Colombo after a business trip, came running to my house as soon he heard the news.

"Paul, are you so crazy to leave the town in such a hurry without any good, tangible reasons?"

"The tsunami, which almost destroyed the town and my house and property, and the likelihood of similar disasters arising out of global warming prompt me to move out of the town. Otherwise, I have no problems at all."

"Haven't you heard the old saying 'Prevention is better than cure'? We will take all the preventive action possible in whatever way we could. I know you are not financially sound and capable of rebuilding the present house where you are living now, as it needs a stronger foundation. I will get your present house demolished entirely and build in its place a house on steel stilts so that it can stand any storm or tidal waves."

"You are a godsend, Newton." I hugged and thanked Newton profusely, and sat with him and the others who had gathered there, including the removalists, to enjoy the occasion over a glass of beer and a hastily prepared barbeque.

Good Intentions, Bad Motives

Nuwara Eliya in Sri Lanka – fondly called "The Little England" – is set against beautiful backdrops of mountains, valleys, waterfalls and lush tea plantations. It is one of the coolest places in the Island, reminiscent of an English spring day, although the temperature drops at night. All around Nuwara Eliya, there is evidence of British settlement. Houses are like country cottages of Queen Ann style mansions.

It was in the remotest part of this health resort an orphanage "Karuna" was started in a dilapidated house for the care of orphans, neglected or abandoned children with the primary intention of giving over children to parents from overseas countries for adoption. It was run by a middle-aged lady called Rosalin de Almeida with Henry Fernando as the Manager of the institution.

Because of the social stigma attached to children born out of wedlock, the orphanage soon became a haven and a boon for single mothers who were prepared to keep their children for custodial care in the orphanage, after signing papers disclosing the identity of the mother and other relevant information. The management kept the papers in a securely locked iron safe. But, it had other ideas.

There were no uniform adoption laws, and the potential parents from overseas countries could select a child for adoption from any orphanage or children's home and file an application for an adoption order in the Magistrate's Court in Colombo, the capital city of Sri Lanka, with the support of the Department of Probation and Child Care Services.

The absence of strict rules governing inter-country adoptions often led to trafficking of children by unscrupulous brokers or middle-men and even by legitimate potential adoptive parents, leading to bribery and corruption.

The main objective of the management of the Karuna Orphanage was to make money by giving children for adoption.

Rosalin de Almeida found giving children for overseas adoptions was a thriving business, as couples from overseas countries would pay any amount of money to get matters expedited. Rosalin, on the other hand, throwing away the traditional principle that adoptions should be in the best interests of the child, did not pay much attention to the suitability of adoptive parents nor concerned whether the child was an orphan or the birth parent was agreeable to the release of the child for overseas adoption.

Henry, the Manager, was a habitual drunkard who was after bottles of whiskey, which adoptive parents bought from duty free liquor stores at the airport. They were given to him as presents. Whiskey was dear and expensive, and beyond the ordinary reach of local people.

The orphanage was equally dirty, ill equipped and understaffed considering the number of inmates. It looked more or less like a juvenile prison or a punishment camp, lacking discipline and control over inmates with the boisterous, older inmates having their day.

With prior arrangement, a rich young couple arrived at the Orphanage to see the child earmarked for adoption. The eight-year-old Madduma Bandara wore a new tracksuit. With neatly combed hair and his inborn broad smile he looked glamorous to capture the hearts of anyone. The Orphanage was decorated for the occasion and flower vases sat on the half-walls and tables.

The couple arrived at the appointed time and Rosalin and Henry were there to welcome them.

"Good morning. You are welcome," said Rosalin, having a subtle glance at the gifts they had brought. "This is Henry, the Manager of the Orphanage." The couple shook hands with both of them who were led to the lounge where Madduma Bandara was waiting to see his potential parents.

As they sat, the couple saw the child, and they really liked him. They gave him a hug and stroked his head as he left the lounge room. They also gave him a parcel of presents, which the older inmates would invariably take peacefully or forcefully later on.

Rosalin then led her to the office room to finalize the transaction. They signed the papers, and while accepting their copy, the couple handed over a cheque for US$5000 towards the building fund as agreed upon earlier.

After tea with them, the couple left the Orphanage.

Madduma Bandara was happy but the thought whether he would be brought up with love, care and security in Australia pricked his tender mind quite often.

The incident, when the birth mother of Kingsley - a close friend of Madduma Bandara who was also an inmate – one day came to see him but was told that he was adopted and taken to Sweden by the adoptive parents.

She made an uproar, and confusion prevailed. When Rosalin, who happened to be in her office at the time, came and led her to the office.

There was hardly any commotion thereafter and the inmates thought that she gave her money to keep her silence.

This incident too made Madduma Bandara nervous whether his own mother would come to see him after he had gone to Australia. The more he thought about them, the more he became agitated.

Most of the inmates advised Madduma Bandara to go ahead with the adoption lest their chances would become less, but he was determined to get out of this prison. He was also not sure what would befall on him in a country like Australia unknown to him.

However, the nagging question was that, despite the prospects of a happy and secure family home in Australia, whether the birth mother could look after him well to bring him up as a productive and good citizen if he remained at home..

An older girl in the Orphanage, Sylvia, liked Madduma Bandara so much, she thought it was the most opportune time to help him out. She taught him some elementary lessons in Sinhala reading and writing so that he could read the agreement signed by his mother and the Orphanage and find out his mother's name and address.

One evening both of them were able to steal the office and safe keys and keep them under their pillows till the night.

When the lights were off and it was dark, Madduma Bandara crept into the office and opened the safe. He was able to trace the papers easily as the names of the parents and their addresses were printed in block letters on the face of the packet. He wrote the name and address of the mother on a scrap paper he took with him, closed the safe and office, kept the keys in the place they were, and came out of the office to the joy and delight of Sylvia who had an eye on Madduma Bandara during the operation from a reasonable distance. The mother's name was Mary de Silva and the address was 185/15, Colombo Road, Kadawata.

Sylvia planned that Madduma Bandara should get out of the Orphanage soon and go in search of his mother. She got a street map of Kadawata and showed him the route. He had to take a bus to Colombo Central Bus Stand and then get a bus to Kadawata from there. She also gave him five Rs10 notes for expenses.

Madduma Bandara was in Kadawata after two hours. He got down at the Kadawata bus stand and was looking for the road on the map when a speeding truck knocked him down. He became unconscious, and died almost instantly, murmuring in inaudible tone, saying, O-h m-y mo-t-h-e-r, O -h, m-y – m-o – t – h – e – r."

Deception

Chaudri was a smart, beautiful 18-year old girl who worked as a receptionist in a pharmacy in Wellington where she lived with her widowed mother. They had a modest income, frugal in spending and were able to keep their heads above water. Chaudri's wages supplemented the meagre income her mother earned from investment in shares and property.

Chaudri was extremely attractive with glittering blue eyes. Above all, her modesty, virtuousness and the flickering half smile coming right from her heart, hovering over her wine-red lips and downplaying the smile of Mona Lisa, attracted customers to the pharmacy more than the drugs and other merchandise offered for sale at discount prices.

Her beauty was the talk of the town, and there were many youngsters who wanted to win over her arms.

Tony Sidman, a 25- year old real estate broker who walked into the pharmacy to buy a packet of Panadol to ease his constant headache was struck by Chaudri's beauty like lightning. Their eyes met directly and they clicked instantly to the joy of both.

"Madam, may I know your name," said a bewildered Tony to Chaudri who was seated at the reception desk.

"Chaudri", she replied with her invasive half smile.

"Where do you live?"

"Just five streets away."

"Your telephone number?"

"8257985."

Tony was so taken up by Chaudri, he could not get a sound sleep for several days. He would roll on the bed with his head buried in the soft pillow, imagining as if he was in Chaudri's arms.

Suddenly he got up from the bed, and rang Chaudri.

"I want to propose myself to you. What do you say?"

"It's quite all right. I love you," came the reply from Chaudri.

They got married and started living together. Tony, who had been struggling in managing his expenditure and was almost in debt, soon found Chaudri a great asset who so frugally kept the household expenditure in check, leaving a considerable balance at the end of each month.

Like an excited child, Chaudri would play with Tony, fondle him, tickle him, and throw herself into Tony's arms and kiss him passionately. Though married for only a couple of months, Tony felt as if they were just now spending the honeymoon.

Chaudri had an insatiable craving for imitation jewellery much to the resentment of Tony who disliked deception in any form. But he ignored Chaudri's hobby, as she was a fabulous wife.

Whenever Chaudri went shopping, she never forgot to buy an imitation necklace, earring or a ring. One day as she returned from a shopping spree, Chaudri placed a necklace on Tony's neck and said, "Dear, don't you like the necklace. It is so elegant and delicate that no one would ever think that it is an imitation."

"Yes, marvellous craftsmanship. It would look better on your neat neck than mine. But I dislike deception."

"Here, no one is deceiving anyone else. It is imitation glass not brilliants or diamonds. When anyone buys it, he/ she would know that it is an imitation, considering the price and the testimony of the shopkeeper. So, there is hardly any deception. In any case, it is my hobby, and I take so much of pleasure and satisfaction in what I do. I do not think I can change my habit at this stage."

"Okay, okay darling," said Tony who hugged and gave her a long kiss, which she enjoyed as if she was wearing a gold ring studded with a brilliant on her shining lip.

In a flash car accident, Chaudri died unexpectedly, a few weeks afterwards. The sudden death of Chaudri upset Tony so much that he did not even go to work regularly. Most of the time he was confined to his room going through the photo albums of Chaudri with teary eyes, and often sobbing.

Tony, to his utter dismay, found he was running short of money and might not be able to balance the budget till the next payday.

He went to Chaudri's room, opened her iron safe where she kept her jewellery and other valuables. He opened the bag in which jewellery was kept and took out the most elegant and delicate necklace to get even a few dollars by selling it.

Tony pocketed the necklace safely and walked into a jewellery shop close to his workplace.

"Good day, Sir. We have got a new shipment of jewellery and other household ornaments offered for sale at very cheap prices to commemorate the 50th anniversary of our shop. Hurry Sir, do not miss the chance."

"It' nice of you, but I have come to sell one of the necklaces of my wife who died recently." Tony would not, however, look at the face of the shopkeeper directly as he felt it was unfair and below his dignity to sell a cheap, deceptive imitation even for a few dollars. Nonetheless, he realized the urgency of making some money now was far greater and more important than the dignity, which no one, even he, could see.

"Okay Sir, let us see the necklace."

Tony took the necklace out and kept it on the table, partly covering his face with the hand, as if he was putting his hair in place.

The shopkeeper weighed the necklace and whispered something inaudible to his Assistant.

"Sir, we can offer you $15,000 because of its good workmanship."

Tony was flabbergasted and lost for words. Looking at the shopkeeper with wide-open eyes, he said, "I will think over it."

"Sir, if you feel that the price we offered is too low, you can get it valued by another jeweller, and we will offer you the same amount with $250 as a bonus.

Tony felt that there was something fishy about the whole transaction. He pocketed the necklace and told the jeweller that he would get in touch with him later.

Tony walked into another jewellery shop with a broad smile across his face. When the shopkeeper saw the necklace, he recognized that he had sold it. He referred up the bill book and told Tony, "Sir, one Chaudri Sidman had bought this necklace about six years back for 17,500. I will offer you $17,000."

"It's OK," said Tony, trying to conceal his big smile.

"Sir, have you got any evidence to show that you are the owner of the necklace."

"Yes, she was my wife who died recently. This is her national identity card and this is mine. The address is the same."

"I believe you, Sir. Here is a cheque for $17,000."

Tony could not believe for a moment that such a fortune had come his way. He thought that it was simply a godsend. He thanked the shopkeeper and left the shop in high spirits.

Within a few weeks, Tony sold the entire collection of jewellery − 11 necklaces, 26 sets of earrings and 15 rings, and realized $290,000 by the sale. He was now a wealthy man. He spent most of his time in pubs and hotels, drinking expensive wines and having lavish dinners with a few of his colleagues in office. While having dinner in a hotel with his friends, one of his closest friends Peter asked him why he was wasting his time in the real estate agency where work was irregular and the sales dwindling.

"Yes Peter, I was thinking of that move last night. With so much of money in my hands, why should I work like a slave to make money for others? Yes, I will meet the boss tomorrow and hand in my resignation."

On the following morning, Tony wrote the letter of resignation, and wearing a stylish suit and a tie to match, he walked in to the office and met the Manager and told him.

"Mr Karapincha, I inherited a fortune of $350,000. I want to start my own business. Here is my letter of resignation with immediate effect." Tony handed over the letter to the Manager, shook his hands and left the office, winking at some of his colleagues who were working.

There were a lot of girls in the town who went after him. He selected a fashionable pretty girl and lived with her for a couple of months. He found her to be modest and good but she was an alcoholic with a persistent nasty cough. She was no match for Chaudri in any respect. Finally, the girl left, to the great relief of Tony.

Tony could not still keep out the thoughts about his darling Chaudri whom he missed badly except in his dreams. In fact, in a dream, he saw Chaudri coming to him like an angel, and started hugging and kissing him as never seen before. Tony was awakened by the dream, sat on the bed deeply moved and started to think what the dream was all about.

Tony got up early in the morning, dressed up neatly and went to a Travel Agency. He booked a cruise round the world, and left two days later in search of a girl to take the place of Chaudri both in form and loving characteristics.

A Costly Drive

Tinado and Tranalene stopped their car on the edge of a cliff and watched the glorious sunset against the background of a dark red sky as various colours came and vanished, giving rise to another colour. It resembled a box of pastel colours a girl had strewn on the canvas in her attempt at colouring.

They looked at the sea hundreds of meters below. The waves were smashing against the face of the cliff giving, at times, a horrible noise as darkness enwrapped them gradually.

"Oh darling, it's too late. It is getting dark. We will have to hurry," said Tinado, caressing Tranalene's head of jet-black hair.

'She is beautiful, sweet with apple-coloured rosy cheeks, glittering eyes, long curly hair and an enchanting smile. She is a treasure.' These were the thoughts that crossed Tinado's mind, made possible by an on-rush of adrenalin.

They got into the car and were on their way. They stopped at a wayside kiosk, and bought some snacks and soft drinks enough for dinner and breakfast.

As they drove away, they came up to a stream where they parked the car under a shady tree to prevent mist from falling on the car.

Tinado went to the stream and took a dip in the icy cold water, which really refreshed him from a long drive. Then he took out the tent, set it up and lit a bonfire to keep them warm.

Tranalene relaxed in a camp bed inside the tent and soon fell asleep.

The beautiful, rising full moon covering her delicate face with a silky cloth to keep her away from the cold, peeped now and then producing a flash of light as if to show Tinado the way to the forest close by.

Tinado entered the forest, and admired the moonbeams flowing through the thick foliage to embrace the earth, a few hare coming their way and disappearing like lightning, and a herd of spotted deer with their charm and innocence stared at Tinado for a while and went on their way.

Suddenly, there was a bang. Tinado looked back and there was nothing.

He took a few steps more and there was yet another blast. He knew it was a gunshot. Curious enough, he looked back more attentively to find three men in full suits struggling with a man who had fallen on the ground. One of them shot him, and he was silenced. The other two also had rifles.

Tinado lost no time, and ran towards the tent, put Taralene up who was fast asleep, and asked to put all her belongings into the car. As soon as the packing was over, they got into the car and Tinado jammed the power pedal, and the car flew like a jet.

However, Tinado looked back through the rear mirror of the car to find that the men in a Ute were following them. They pointed their rifles at the car and fired the first shot. There was a cracking noise, and the rear window was in splinters.

Tinado drove a little further and parked the car on the edge of the road and ran to the forest and hid themselves in the bushes.

With torches flashing, the three men started searching for Tinado and Taralene among the bushes. Soon, one of them spotted Tinado and took him out by the scruff of his neck. As he was about to hit Tinado, Tinado got hold of the head of the assailant and pushed him to the ground. He punched him as hard as he could until he was almost half conscious. He took his rifle and with Taralene ran towards the car.

Both Tinado and Taralene were highly worked up with anger and retribution, as Tinado pressed the accelerator almost to the floor to get ahead of those criminals. They were under a false impression and realized it only when the Ute was seen again tracking them.

Tinado and Taralene ran into the woods once again to save themselves from these heartless criminals who harm innocent people with no reasons at all.

The criminals are more competent in their activities and they could not be outdone. They traced Tinado and Taralene and were pulled out of the bushes one by one.

First, they took Tinado and gave him two punches to the head and he fell unconscious.

Taralene struggled to rid herself, and in the ensuing struggle, she received a punch on her face. She fell on the ground and pretended to be senseless or dead.

The two criminals walked up to Tinado and raised him. He was then handcuffed and tied to a tree.

Then they picked up Taralene and dragged her along the ground as she tried to free herself.

Tinado looked at Taralene with teary eyes, sobbing louder and louder.

Taralene could not do anything except to wave at Tinado, crying and sobbing. She said, "Tina, do not worry. I will be with you eternally though not in flesh but at least in spirits. She gave him a final flying kiss, and vanished as the criminals dragged her into the woods.

Perseverance Pays

Muthu (meaning, Jewel) always enjoyed the waters of the Molapu Oya (river that flows into the sea) just in front of his house. Muthu's local peers, including his best friend Samara, used to bathe in the river and play water games almost daily. There was only one fee levying swimming pool in the town, which was beyond the means of poor local lads.

As they grew up and in higher classes at school, Muthu and Samara used to go to the sea beach in the evenings to work out geometrical sums by drawing diagrams and formulas on the sand beds made to look like a slate by removing the upper layers of sand. The beach was only about 20 kms from Muthu's house. Samara was very keen in mathematics and science while Muthu's main interests were in literature and history, his favorite subjects.

As the sea beach becomes crowded when the afternoon wears out and the sun set draws near, it becomes increasingly crowded as locals as well tourists assemble there to watch the Molapu Oya flows into the ocean with a clear blue sky as the background, providing a very spectacular sight. People used to call it the "Waters Meet".

This spot is just by the side of the town's popular sea resort. It is a body of large shallow water enclosed by a reef decorated with layers of multi-coloured corals – a safe home for the countless number of coloured fish. Visitors in glass-bottomed boats cruise around the reef and watch the attractive corals and fish at very close range. Boat trips were expensive and the ordinary people could not afford them.

It was one of the tourists' attractions in the region, besides providing facilities for surfing, snorkelling and diving.

Muthu, Samara and their peers hang around the place, envying those who enjoy the beauty and excitement of the place. They had no money to make any boat trips, and this really saddened and depressed Muthu more than the others. Sometimes, they would purposely avoid watching the activities for days and days.

"Samara, how come some people are born to rich families and the others to poor parents? How is that when Molapu Oya meets the sea, it is totally absorbed by it leaving no identity or any signs of recognition of the Molapu Oya?" These were the questions Muthu posed, but neither Samara nor Muthu had any clear-cut answers to them.

Muthu was born at a time when his parent's copra and coir-yarn industry was at low ebb as a result of the Great Depression of the 1920s. Verdicts in several civil law suits about temporary land holding went against them, requiring them to pay compensation and costs of action to the plaintiffs. Muthus's childhood years were dreary, and he was denied of toys and play materials in comparison with the other children in the neighbourhood.

At the age of five, Muthu was enrolled as a student at the local school where the medium of instruction was his mother tongue, Sinhala. At the same time, his parents took him to the Buddhist temple of the village and arranged for him to learn both Sinhala and Pali from the High Priest who was from a closely connected family of Muthu's parents. The High Priest found Muthu to be an intelligent and talented pupil and paid extra attention to his studies.

On the first day he went to the temple, the High Priest asked Muthu what his father was doing now.

"Reverend Sir, he is now seated on the footsteps to the temple to take me back home after my lessons," came the reply like a bullet.

The High Priest was surprised how alert and talented he was, realizing that he did not make the question clearer to him, although he was trying to find out his father's job.

Whenever Muthu did an exercise in his studies well, the High Priest used to give him a bunch of grapes in recognition of his good work. Grapes were rare and expensive at the time and were out of reach for the ordinary. He now liked the temple and his studies even more and never missed a single Sunday. It was on Sundays only that he went to the temple for studies. He even became an active member of the Children's Society formed by children in the village to work for the welfare of the temple.

On Poya (Full Moon) days, it is customary for Buddhists to visit their temples and pay homage to the Buddha and listen to sermons, and take part in religious talks, especially in the evenings. The entire family members, including children, would attend religious rites conducted by priests throughout the day.

Muthu, with the other members of the society, would go to the temple in advance to help elders make arrangements for the day. Sometimes it became a trying time for Muthu to discipline the children as most of them play about in the temple premises when their parents listened to sermons indoors.

The temple was situated on a hillock. The leafy, shady trees around the temple premises covered the entire temple except the dome of the dagoba, which could be seen from the distance like the crest of a peacock. When the pinnacle was illuminated with thousands of tiny electric globes, it presented a spectacular, heart-throbbing sight.

There were about 50 stone steps, splendidly carved with great skill, leading to the temple. On each side there were two concrete beams with polished surfaces connecting the steps and sloping downwards to the ground. Children used to slide on them, some being successful and a few others falling to the turf below. Though a holy day and a holy place, playful children would turn that part of the premises to a circus ground, sliding down the beam like tiny acrobats.

The pool in the premises studded with full blown white lotus flowers where two or three coloured ping-pong balls would repeatedly rise towards the sky and come down as quickly as they went up by the force of automatic taps fixed in the pool. This kept children glued to the pool, excitingly watching the drama. This, in fact, eased the work of Muthu

Muthu, a silent spectator and having an eye on the behaviour of children, would softly exercise his authority to discipline them if they faulted. He relished in the confidence and responsibility given to him by the High Priest and fulfilled the guardianship role to the satisfaction of both the priests and the elders. Children also appreciated the work he did by giving him snack bars and chocolates quite often as presents.

When Muthu was in secondary school, his parents could not pay his school fees regularly and they ran into arrears. The Principal sent a letter to the parents, debarring Muthu from attending school until the arrears were paid up.

Muthu was greatly incensed and upset over it that he cried for days and days even refusing to eat food. Determined as he was, Muthu walked into the office of the Principal and appealed for reinstatement. Considering his excellent records of studies provided by the class teachers, Muthu was allowed to attend classes again, and the monthly school fee of Rupees 5 was reduced to Rupees 2.50. He was so delighted that he ran home and broke the news to his parents who hugged him and gave him a shirt as a present.

Muthu's studiousness, his intelligence and smartness attracted several girls in the school towards him. There was always competition for him from the girls. He actually fell in love with the most beautiful and attractive of the lot. Their relationship grew fast secretively as, at the time, intimate relationships with boys and girls were looked down upon by both teachers and elders. Muthu and her girlfriend Yasodhara would hide themselves behind a school cupboard and steal a kiss as opportunity arose. His relationship kept him away from his studies resulting in being able to secure only the third position in the class at the term test. This disturbed Muthu and he was upset because that was the first time in his school life he slipped to the third position. But he was determined to regain his usual position in the next test on the advice of his girlfriend and Samara, his best friend.

Samara had other ideas and he went after the girl and formed a relationship with her without the knowledge of Muthu. Muthu became aware of the relationship but he ignored it and devoted his time to studies and did not even bother to admonish Samara or Yasodhara.

Years passed by. Muthu left the school after passing Year 10 and joined the public service as a clerk. With the savings he made, he started studying for the GCE (Advanced Level) examination of the University of London as an external student at a private evening school. He passed the examination but could not proceed further as the government banned holding of overseas examinations because of the country's financial stringency. Upset by this, he turned his attention to another girl in the office who worked as a stenographer. She was very smart, attractive and beautiful. She was westernized and stood out over the other girls in the office. Muthu from a country town, though playful, was modest and shy. But the relationship did not last long as Muthu's parents proposed a girl of their choice to him. This arrangement came as a blessing in disguise for Muthu, as he was not really keen about the affair. He met the girl his parents had proposed and agreed to marry her as she was from an established family with considerable wealth.

The government changed, and with it commenced the holding of overseas examinations once again. While preparing himself for a degree of the University of London, he started writing short stories, poems and articles on current topics to newspapers and magazines, which became very popular. He passed the examination with Honours.

Later, Muthu migrated to an overseas country with his wife and two children. He settled down well in the new country and in the job as an administrator of a welfare agency. He studied further and obtained several graduate diplomas in journalism and also obtained a Master's degree in writing. He continued his hobby of writing articles to papers without slowing down.

Subsequently, Muthu applied for a course to study for a Doctorate in Creative Writing. He got it. With his hands above his head like an excited child, he yelled out saying, "over the moon."

Hello Dolly

Oh Dolly, what a beauty you are
Big boobs and fleshy buttocks!
Like mother like daughter.
How it happened we like to know?
I was cloned from mum's mammary gland
Both alike, it's no surprise.
Friends giggle when they
Mistake me for mum.
Depressed I'm, my self-respect and dignity in thin air
With nowhere to go, I just roam.
How come people call you Dolly?
It's after Dolly Parton, the singer with over-sized boobs,
But I do not care two hoots.
Who created you Dolly dear?
It's scientists I hear.
Oh God! Man created animals!
It takes me out of my roots,
No wonder.
Just tell me then, who created man and woman?
It's God people say
Man from ashes and woman from his rib,
Isn't it funny dear?
No wonder.
Is God then a man?

Who knows, no one has sighted him,
And God is not here to question,
But some say "yes" and some say "no"
Skeptical are people on this issue,
No wonder.

About the Author

The author was a professional and social work educator in Sr Lanka. He migrated to Australia in 1975 as a member of the Australian Association of Social Workers. He worked as a Senior Social Worker in Federal and State departments, holding higher positions in welfare agencies and institutions involved in childcare.

As an administrator, he was responsible for placing over 500 orphaned and neglected children from Thailand, the Philippines, South Korea, India, and Sri Lanka, and from Vietnam after the fall of Saigon. The majority of children fitted in well into the Australian society.

The author is a versatile writer and has contributed a series of articles and letters to leading national newspapers, community papers and magazines both in Sri Lanka and South Australia.

He retired from the public service and has settled down in South Australia, now practising as a writer, author and journalist.

The author has an Honours degree in Philosophy from the University of London, a Diploma in Social Work (Sri Lanka), a Special Certificate in Advanced Social Work (Philippines), a Higher Diploma in Advanced Freelance Journalism (Australia), a Master of Letters (Australia) and a PhD in Creative Writing (Ireland).